I want spaghetti!

This edition first published in 2015 by Gecko Press
PO Box 9335, Marion Square, Wellington 6141, New Zealand
info@geckopress.com

Distributed in New Zealand by Upstart Distribution, www.upstartpress.co.nz
Distributed in Australia by Scholastic Australia, www.scholastic.com.au
Distributed in the UK by Bounce Sales & Marketing, www.bouncemarketing.co.uk

Original title: *Je veux des pâtes !*
Text and illustrations by Stephanie Blake

A catalogue record for this book is available from the National Library of New Zealand.

Translated by Linda Burgess
Edited by Penelope Todd
Typeset by Vida & Luke Kelly, New Zealand
Printed in China by Everbest Printing Co. Ltd, an accredited ISO 14001 & FSC certified printer

ISBN hardback: 978-1-927271-91-9
ISBN paperback: 978-1-927271-92-6

For more curiously good books, visit www.geckopress.com

Stephanie Blake

I want spaghetti!

GECKO PRESS

Once
there was
a little rabbit
who would
only eat
one
thing...

Spaghetti!

At breakfast time
when his mother said,
"Come and eat your toast,
my little rabbit,"
he replied,

"Yuck!

It's horrible.
I won't eat it!"

At lunchtime
when his father said,
"Come and eat your
sandwiches,
my little rabbit,"
he replied,
"No! I want spaghetti."

PLEASE MAKE HIM SOME SPAGHETTI!
SPAGHETTI

At dinner time
when his mother said,
"Eat your soup,
my little rabbit,"
he replied,
"YuckthissoupisDISGUSTING."

"That's enough!"
said his mother.
"Go to your room."

In a

tiny,

tiny

little

voice,

he said,

“I want spaghetti.”

I want spaghetti.

I want spaghetti.

I want spaghetti!

I

WANT

SPAGHETTI!

Slam! Crash! Bang!

"ALL
I WANT
IS
SPAGHETTI!"

Then Simon heard
his mother say to his father,
“Darling, this chocolate cake
is exquisite.”

Simon cried out:

“But I want
chocolate cake too!”

His mother said,
“Come and eat your soup,
my little rabbit,
and then you can have
chocolate cake!”

And that’s exactly what he did.

The next day
at lunchtime
his father said,
"Come and eat your spaghetti,
my little rabbit."

Simon replied:

“I
want…
SAUSAGES!”